Lisa and
the Gronk

Written and
illustrated by

PATRICIA COOMBS

Lisa and the Grompet

A YEARLING BOOK

Published by
Dell Publishing Co., Inc.
1 Dag Hammarskjold Plaza
New York, New York 10017

Yearling ® TM 913705, Dell Publishing Co., Inc.

ISBN: 0-440-44892-1

Reprinted by arrangement with Lothrop, Lee and Shepard Co.
Printed in the United States of America
Second Dell Printing—November 1980
FL

Once upon a time, about a week, or
maybe a year ago a little girl named Lisa
got tired of being told what to do.

Lisa woke up that morning and her big
sister said:
"Don't make so much noise.
Don't shut the window.
Don't bang the shade.
Don't knock over the goldfish bowl."

Lisa went downstairs. Her mother said:
"Don't wear that old shirt.
And pull up your socks.
And don't forget you have a piano lesson today."

And her father said:
"Don't step in the dog's dish.
And pull up your socks."
He went off to work and forgot to say
goodbye.

11

Lisa sat down to eat her breakfast.

"Sit down and eat your breakfast," said her mother. "Take your vitamin pill and don't spill the milk."

Lisa got crosser and crosser. She gave her vitamin pill to the dog. The dog spit it out.

"I'm tired of being told what to do," said Lisa, and she went outside.

"Every day everybody tells me what to do. I don't like it. I will go away all by myself. I will tell my own self what to do."

And she did.

She walked and walked and walked and walked.

Lisa looked at the flowers in bloom.

"Nobody says, 'Don't forget to bloom tomorrow. Don't forget to wiggle your roots and grow a new leaf because a bug ate one yesterday.' "

Lisa looked at the butterflies flying around her.

"Nobody says, 'Don't sit on that flower! Sit on the other one!' Butterflies don't yell."

Lisa walked and walked. She looked back down the path. She couldn't see her house anymore.

"There," said Lisa. "I have run away."
She sat down to rest and think about
things.

Lisa heard a funny noise. She looked all around. She did not see anything.

Then something pinched her.

"Ow!" said Lisa.

She looked down. Something very small was making a popping sound and jumping up and down.

"What are you?" asked Lisa.

"A grompet. A grompet. A grompet!" yelled the grompet. "You sat on my front yard and squashed it."

"I'm sorry," said Lisa. "I didn't know it was your front yard."

"Well it was. And you squashed it. Don't forget to LOOK before you sit down!"

Lisa sighed and looked at the grompet. "You sound like my mother."

The grompet came up close and looked at Lisa. Lisa looked at the grompet.

"NOW what did I do?" said Lisa. "I told you I was sorry I squashed your front yard."

"When you squash somebody's front yard,
the least you can do is to ask them to tell
you the story of their life."

"I'm sorry," said Lisa. "I didn't know I was supposed to ask you the story of your life."

"You sound like my Uncle George!" shouted the grompet. And he burst into tears.

"Poor Grompet," said Lisa. "I know how you feel. I am running away because I am always being told what to do. It makes me mad and sad, and everything smashes and spills, and everybody yells."

The grompet stopped crying. "Don't tell me the story of YOUR life," he yelled.

"I'm sorry," said Lisa.

"All right then," said the grompet. "I'll tell you mine. My Uncle George never told me to eat my breakfast or pull up my socks or take my vitamin pill. He didn't tell me to do anything. So I just stood there and shrank."

"Really?" said Lisa. "I would like that."

The grompet frowned. "You would like to stand around and shrink?"

"Of course not," said Lisa. "I meant . . . oh, never mind. Tell me more."

"I was afraid I would shrink into Nothing At All," the grompet went on. "So I ran away. Nobody told me to go home, so I never did. All I know is I am a grompet and I am very small and very sad."

They both sat thinking. Then Lisa said, "Everybody tells me what to do and I don't like it."

The grompet came closer. He looked at Lisa, and Lisa looked at him.

"Would you like to tell me what to do?" whispered the grompet.

"Oh, yes! What a wonderful idea!" Lisa jumped up, and . . .

"NOW look what you've done!" shouted the grompet. He had tumbled over and was stuck under a mushroom.

Lisa started to help the grompet up, but she changed her mind. She frowned at him instead.

"Don't be silly!" she scolded. "Get out from under that mushroom right now. And don't forget to brush yourself off."

The grompet stopped looking angry and began to smile. He smiled and smiled.

He crawled out from under the mushroom and brushed himself off.

He came over to Lisa. Lisa picked him up and sat him on her knee. She picked a leaf out of his beard for him.

The grompet smiled.

Lisa smiled, too.

"I love you," said the grompet.

"And I love you," said Lisa. "I'll take you home with me and take care of you. I'll tell you what to do all the time."

"And I'll be happy," said the grompet. "I'll never ever shrink into Nothing At All!"

"That's right," said Lisa. "Sit on my shoulder. We are going home for lunch. After lunch we have a piano lesson. Don't forget."

Lisa and the grompet skipped back along the path through the flowers and the butterflies.

They got home just as Lisa's mother was saying, "Lisa! Wash your hands and face. Lunch is ready. Hurry up!"

"Yes, Mother," said Lisa.

She went upstairs and put the grompet beside the washbowl.

"Wash your wings and face, Grompet," she said. "And don't forget behind your ears."

The grompet washed his wings and face and behind his ears, and Lisa helped him dry off.

Lisa put him back on her shoulder and they went downstairs.

Lisa and the grompet had soup and peanut butter sandwiches for lunch.

"Don't get your beard in the soup or the soup in your beard, Grompet," said Lisa.

The grompet was so happy he ate all his lunch.

Lisa was so happy she ate all her lunch. And she didn't spill a thing.

After lunch Lisa and the grompet sat down at the piano.

"Be very still, Grompet," said Lisa, "while I practice."

The grompet smiled.

"I love you," he said.

"I love you," said Lisa, and she began to play.

MS READ-a-thon—
a simple way to start
youngsters reading

Boys and girls between 6 and 14 can join the MS READ-a-thon and help find a cure for Multiple Sclerosis by reading books. And they get two rewards — the enjoyment of reading, and the great feeling that comes from helping others.

Parents and educators: For complete information call your local MS chapter. Or mail the coupon below.

Kids can help, too!